ilience
AF584836

POO POO

happens!

written,
illustrated &
designed
by
trace moroney

Poo poo (a.k.a. bad stuff) happens and things go wrong.

It may be because of something I have done ... or not done,
or because of something someone else has done,
or ... bad stuff can happen for no reason at all.

But one thing is for sure ... poo poo happens to us all!

a.k.a. means:
'also known as'.
Or another word that
means the same.

Poo poo – or bad stuff – is another way to describe problems, setbacks, mistakes, failures, tough times, challenges, stressful situations, tragedy, threats, illness, or life changes ... like ...

hurting your toe, starting a new school, not doing well at something, or when a new family member arrives!

Or more serious things like being bullied or hurt, parents arguing or a broken home, or someone you love has died.

HOME
SWEET
HOME

Sometimes the poo poo
is small ...

and ... sometimes it is ginormous
and stinky and feels too big to cope with.

It is kind to remember: different people respond
to the same problem in different ways.
So, what may feel like a small problem for you –
could feel like a **big** problem for someone else.

Being able to cope in a positive way and bounce back, again and again, after every setback is called

resilience.

Being resilient is not something we are born with, but something we ***learn*** each time we have managed a problem in a healthy and positive way.

EMERGENCY
SURVIVAL KIT

You can't always control when poo poo happens, but you ***can*** control how you behave or react when it does.

Being resilient doesn't mean that you won't experience difficult problems in the future - BUT - you ***can*** get better at coping with them and learn positive ways to help you become a stronger and more awesome YOU!

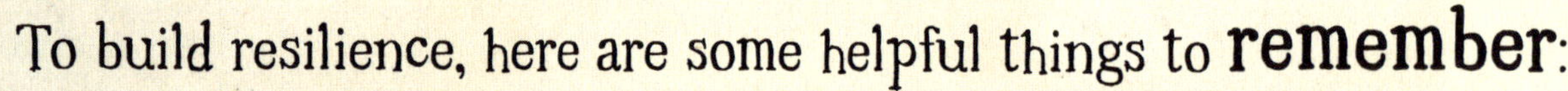

To build resilience, here are some helpful things to **remember**:

POO POO happens to everyone!

EVERYONE experiences problems, setbacks, or stressful situations.

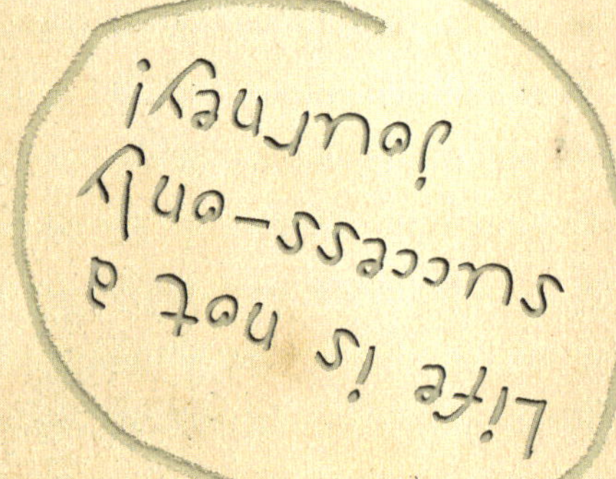

Resilience grows a little bit each time you overcome a problem in a positive way.

Being resilient helps you understand most problems don't last forever.
Think of problems as exercise for your brain ... the more problems you manage well - the stronger and more resilient you become.
You are not alone.
Share your worries with someone you trust, and ask for help if you need it.
If you didn't have bad days - how would you know when you were having a good one?

And ...

It can feel easier to want to
run away from a problem ...
but most of the time
it follows you and
doesn't go away!

Try to be brave,
accept there is a problem,
and imagine saying to it ...

Hey, you big p...
roblem! I am going to
find a way to cope
with you - and
I'm going to be
OK!

To build resilience, here are some helpful things to **have**:

A supportive adult

This is a grown-up you trust, who is a good role model, a good listener, reliable, someone you feel comfortable sharing your problems with, and who supports you.

A supportive family

Helps you feel accepted, loved, supported, and that you belong.

A positive attitude

Try to think of something good that could come out of the problem – even if it is that you coped with it really well.

Self-esteem

What you think, feel, and believe about yourself in a positive way.

Humour

Sometimes it helps to find something funny in a difficult situation and have a good laugh!

Good friends
t could be just one, or it could be a bunch - but good friends accept you for just being you and help you realise that you are not alone.
Empathy
Understanding how someone else may feel, and seeing things from their point of view.
Self-belief
Believe that you will cope with the problem, you will learn from it, you will be OK ... and ... may be even stronger than before!
Kindness
Being able to feel kindness toward yourself and show it to others.
An open mind
This means feeling ready to accept change, and brave enough to think about different ways to manage or solve problems.

To build resilience, here are some helpful things to **do**:

Talk about your problem with a supportive grown-up, and share your thoughts and feelings.
It is normal and ok to feel sad, scared, anxious, or angry when you are dealing with a difficult situation.
Talk about different ideas that could help you work through your problem in a healthy and positive way.

Take care of you. Try to sleep well, eat healthy food, and exercise every day. This helps you feel strong and have more energy to cope with problems - and can make some of the stress go away.

And ...

Make a list of the things you really like about yourself, the things you love to do, and the things you are thankful for. Remember these positive things – especially when you are struggling with a problem or negative thoughts and feelings.

And have a special calm, **peaceful place** where you feel safe to go to if you need a break.

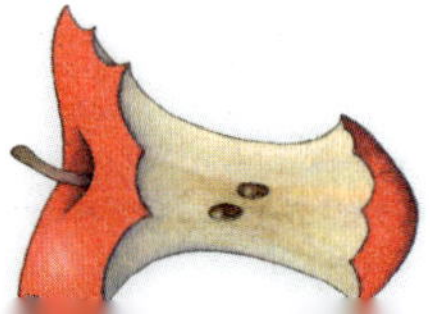

I love sailing
I love my dog
I really like being me
I am thankful for my family
I am thankful for this special tree
I am thankful for my friends

my POO POO scale

Sometimes, a problem can feel much, **much** bigger than it really is.
Each time you have a problem, use this Poo Poo Scale to help you work out how big your problem feels to **you**.
Try to be realistic about how big your problem is ... which can be *really* hard to do!

Number 1 is a small, annoying problem ...
and number 10 is the biggest, stinkiest,
worst, most serious problem!

So ... how big is your problem?

Having a plan can help you feel in control of your feelings and reactions to a problem.

Each time you have a problem, work through each step of the Poo Poo Plan. Writing your answers to these questions will help you deal with the problem in a way that is more kind and calming for **you**.

Remember: You cannot change other people's behaviour … only your own.

You can download and print My Poo Poo Plan at: www.tracemoroney.com

my POO POO plan

1. My problem is:

2. On the Poo Poo Scale, the size of my problem is (circle):
   1 2 3 4 5 6 7 8 9 10

3. These are the things I **can't** control:

4. These are the things I **can** control:

5. Something I can change to make things better:

6. The person or people I can talk to or ask for help:

7. Something I can learn from this:

8. The outcome that I really hope for is:

9. If I have this problem again, this is what I would do differently:

10. These are the things I have done really well:

Next time poo poo happens – I will remember:
the things I managed well last time,
to change the things I didn't manage so well,
the new coping skills I learned,
and ... to make a Poo Poo Plan.

Each time I overcome a problem, I feel stronger and more confident – so that next time poo poo happens, I feel better able to cope and bounce back!

Notes to parents and caregivers

When the poo poo hits the fan (so to speak), how do you handle it? Do you blame yourself or others, or do you throw a tantrum ... or do you calmly assess and respond in a considered way? We ***all*** face difficulties, setbacks, adversity, trauma, and other stressors as we learn to navigate our way through life's inevitable ups and downs. Becoming more resilient helps us cope during difficult times, and become more confident and better prepared to deal with future problems.

What is resilience?

Emotional resilience is typically defined as a person's capacity to adapt and grow following adversity. It is the measure of how we cope with things that happen to us, and our capacity to bounce back – again and again – after every challenge.

Resilience is not something we are born with, or simply acquire, but that we learn each time we manage a problem in a healthy and positive way. It is impossible to build resilience without experiencing adversity – and, therefore, building resilience is a life-long journey.

Being more resilient doesn't mean we won't experience difficult problems or circumstances in the future, but it does mean we are better able and willing to work through the recovery process more readily, learn from the experience, and accept that change is inevitable.

Building resilience

Try to imagine the setbacks and challenges you experience as soulful exercises to help build resilience. And, like physical exercise, it takes time, effort, and intent to grow and strengthen our emotional resilience.

Here are some helpful strategies for building your child's resilience:

- **Help build your child's social connections and support network.** Encourage healthy relationships with empathetic peers, and at least one trusted, reliable, and supportive adult (your child's 'go-to person' in times of need) ... often this is likely to be you. Encourage your child to join a group that aligns with their interest/s and enjoyment. Strong and healthy relationships provide the foundation on which resilience is built.
- **Be a good role model.** Your child primarily learns about resilience from watching how you and significant others in their life respond to setbacks and difficult times – so, if they see you deal with a problem in a positive and healthy way, they learn that they can do the same. As parents, we often want to jump in and make everything ok for our child or shield them from disappointment, but it is important for your child to experience uncomfortable feelings and problems so that they can learn to work things out for themselves (of course, with your patience and support). Overcoming small problems helps to build your child's resilience in preparation for bigger challenges.

- **Help your child to keep things in perspective and in context.** We are all familiar with the saying *'don't make a mountain out of a mole-hill'*, but many of us do exactly that! Try to be realistic about the size or severity of the problem. Have your child use the *Poo Poo Scale* in this book to help work out how big the problem is to them. Help your child understand that all problems can be overcome and uncomfortable feelings will pass.
- **Create a plan.** With each problem your child experiences, encourage them to brainstorm possible solutions and write a plan (use the *Poo Poo Plan* in this book). This helps them to identify the things they can control, the things they can't control, and the things they may learn – or do differently next time. Creating a plan helps to view a problem more objectively. Discuss possible outcomes before the plan is activated to ensure the decisive actions are healthy and safe for your child and others.
- **Take care of your child's health and wellbeing.** Encourage exercise, healthy food, drinking water, calming and restful bedtime rituals, and good sleep, and practise mindfulness – all helpful in reducing stress.
- **Help your child understand and accept that change is a natural and inevitable part of life.** Nothing stays the same – from one year to the next, one day to the next, or from one second to the next.
- **Give it another go!** Encourage your child to try again when things haven't worked out the way they wanted them to the first time. No matter the result, praise your child for trying … it takes courage to pick yourself up and give something another go!
- **Focus on the positive stuff!** It is all too easy to let emotions that accompany problems or setbacks overwhelm us. Teach your child awareness of negative thinking – and to shift their focus to the things they really like about themself and the things they love to do … and do more of them! Nurture the positive attributes and abilities in your child … and yourself. Although it is difficult to be optimistic in difficult times, try to be positive and hopeful – and visualise the outcome you would like rather than worrying about the worst, or about things that haven't happened.
- **Praise your child when you see them manage a problem well.** It encourages them to have more confidence when the next problem (or poo poo) happens ... and helps them feel good about who they are!

For more information and support material (including *My Poo Poo Scale* and *My Poo Poo Plan*) visit: **www.tracemoroney.com**

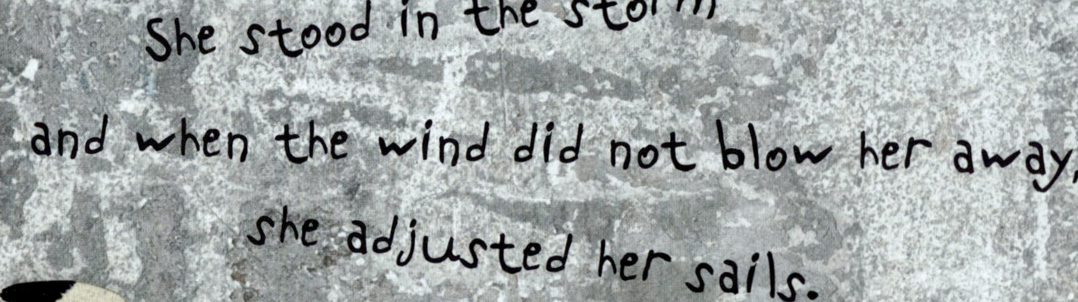

EQ PUBLICATIONS

Published with love by EQ Publications Ltd
email: hello@eqpublications.nz

www.tracemoroney.com
Edited by Madeleine Collinge

Printed in China by
RR Donnelley Asia Printing Solutions Ltd.

First published 2022.